SHANNACH: THE LAST

SHANNACH: THE LAST

by Leigh Brackett

Even in this grip of alien horror a man could not throw away his lifetime goal . . . and not stand idly by as endless rows of alabaster, shapes seated in their chars of stone, thought-rules this gargoyle planet from the dead blackness of deep Mercurian caverns.

I

It was dark in the caves under Mercury. It was hot, and there was no sound in them but the slow plodding of Trevor's heavy boots.

Trevor had been wandering for a long time, lost in this labyrinth where no human being had ever gone before. And Trevor was an angry man. Through no fault or will of his own he was about to die, and he was not ready to die. Moreover, it seemed a wicked thing to come to his final moment here in the stifling dark, buried under alien mountains high as Everest.

He wished now that he had stayed in the valley. Hunger and thirst would have done for him just the same, but at least he would have died in the open like a man, and not like a rat trapped in a drain.

Yet there was not really much to choose between them as a decent place to die. A barren little hell-hole the valley had been, even before the quake, with nothing to draw a man there except the hope of finding sun-stones, one or two of which could transform a prospector into a plutocrat.

Trevor had found no sun-stones. The quake had brought down a whole mountain wall on his ship, leaving him with a pocket torch, a handful of food tablets, a canteen of water, and the scant clothing he stood in.

He had looked at the naked rocks, and the little river frothing green with chemical poisons, and he had gone away into the tunnels, the ancient blowholes of a cooling planet, gambling that he might find a way out of the valleys.

Mercury's Twilight Belt is cut into thousands of cliff-locked pockets, as a honeycomb is cut into cells. There is no way over the mountains, for the atmosphere is shallow, and the jagged peaks stand up into airless space. Trevor knew that only one more such pocket lay between him and the open plains. If he could get to and through that last pocket, he had thought...

But he knew now that he was not going to make it.

He was stripped to the skin already, in the terrible heat. When the weight of his miner's boots became too much to drag, he shed them, padding on over the rough rock with bare feet. He had nothing left now but the torch. When the light went, his last hope went with it.

After a while it went.

The utter blackness of the grave shut down. Trevor stood still, listening to the pulse of his own blood in the silence, looking at that which no man needs a light to see. Then he flung the torch away and stumbled on, driven to fight still by the terror which was greater than his weakness.

Twice he struck against the twisting walls, and fell, and struggled up again. The third time he remained on hands and knees, and crawled.

He crept on, a tiny creature entombed in the bowels of a planet. The bore grew smaller and smaller, tightening around him. From time to time he lost consciousness, and it became increasingly painful to struggle back to an awareness of the heat and the silence and the pressing rock.

After one of these periods of oblivion he began to hear a dull, steady thunder. He could no longer crawl. The bore had shrunk to a mere crack, barely large enough for him to pass through worm-like on his belly. He sensed now a deep, shuddering vibration in the rock.

It grew stronger, terrifying in that enclosed space. Steam slipped wraithlike into the smothering air.

The roar and the vibration grew to an unendurable pitch. Trevor was near to strangling in the steam. He was afraid to go on, but there was no other way to go. Quite suddenly his hands went out into nothingness.

The rock at the lip of the bore must have been rotten with erosion. It gave under his weight and pitched him headfirst into a thundering rush of water that was blistering hot and going somewhere in a great hurry through the dark.

After that Trevor was not sure of anything. There was the scalding heat and the struggle to keep his head up and the terrible speed of the sub-Mercurian river racing on to its destiny. He struck rock several times, and once he held his breath for a whole eternity until the roof of the tunnel rose up again.

He was only dimly aware of a long sliding fall downward through a sudden brightness. It was much cooler. He splashed feebly, because his brain had not told his body to stop, and the water did not fight him.

His feet and hands struck solid bottom. He floundered on, and presently the water was gone. He made one attempt to rise. After that he lay still.

The great mountains leaned away from the Sun. Night came, and with it violent storm and rain. Trevor did not know it. He slept, and when he woke the savage dawn was making the high cliffs flame with white light.

Something was screaming above his head.

Aching and leaden still with exhaustion, he roused up and looked about him.

SHANNACH: THE LAST

He sat on a beach of pale gray sand. At his feet were the shallows of a gray-green lake that filled a stony basin some half-mile in breadth. To his left the underground river poured out of the cliff-face, spreading into a wide, riffling fan of foam. Off to his right, the water spilled over the rim of the basin to become a river again somewhere below, and beyond the rim, veiled in mist and the shadow of a mountain wall, was a valley.

Behind him, crowding to the edge of the sand, were trees and ferns and flowers, alien in shape and color but triumphantly alive. And from what he could see of it, the broad valley was green and riotous with growth. The water was pure, the air had a good smell, and it came to Trevor that he had made it. He was going to live a while longer, after all.

Forgetting his weariness, he sprang up, and the thing that had hissed and screamed above him swooped down and passed the claw tip of a leathery wing so close to his face that it nearly gashed him. He stumbled backward, crying out, and the creature rose in a soaring spiral and swooped again.

Trevor saw a sort of flying lizard, jet black except for a saffron belly. He raised his arms to ward it off, but it did not attack him, and as it swept by he saw something that woke in him amazement, greed, and a peculiarly unpleasant chill of fear.

Around its neck the lizard-thing wore a golden collar. And set into the scaly flesh of its head—into the bone itself, it seemed—was a sun-stone. There was no mistaking that small vicious flash of radiance. Trevor had dreamed of sun-stones too long to be misled. He watched the creature rise again into the steamy sky and shivered, wondering who, or what, had set that priceless thing into the skull of a flying lizard—and why.

It was the *why* that bothered him the most. Sun-stones are not mere adornments for wealthy ladies. They are rare, radioactive crystals, having a half-life one third greater than radium, and are used exclusively in the construction of delicate electronic devices dealing with frequencies above the first octave.

Most of that relatively unexplored superspectrum was still a mystery. And the strangely jeweled and collared creature circling above him filled Trevor with a vast unease.

It was not hunting. It did not wish to kill him. But it made no move to go away.

From far down the valley, muted by distance to a solemn bell note that rolled between the cliffs, Trevor heard the booming of a great song.

A sudden desire for concealment sent him in among the trees. He worked his way along the shore of the lake. Looking up through the branches he saw the black wings lift and turn, following him.

The lizard was watching him with its bright, sharp eyes. It noted the path of his movements through the ferns and flowers, as a hawk watches a rabbit.

He reached the lip of the basin where the water poured over in a cataract several hundred feet high. Climbing around the shoulder of a rocky bastion, Trevor had his first clear look at the valley.

Much of it was still vague with mist. But it was broad and deep, with a sweep of level plain and clumps of forest, locked tight between the barrier mountains. And as he made out other details, Trevor's astonishment grew out of all measure.

The land was under cultivation. There were clusters of thatched huts among the fields, and in the distance was a rock-built city, immense and unmistakable in the burning haze of dawn.

SHANNACH: THE LAST

Trevor crouched there, staring, and the winged lizard swung in lazy circles, watching, waiting, while he tried to think.

A fertile valley such as this was rare enough in itself. But to find fields and a city was beyond belief. He had seen the aboriginal tribes that haunt some of the cliff-locked worlds of the Twilight Belt—sub-human peoples who live precariously among the bitter rocks and boiling springs, hunting the great lizards for food. None of this was ever built by them.

Unless, in this environment, they had advanced beyond the Age of Stone...

The gong sounded again its deep challenging note. Trevor saw the tiny figures of mounted men, no larger than ants at that distance, come down from the city and ride out across the plain.

Relief and joy supplanted speculation in Trevor's mind. He was battered and starving, lost on an alien world, and anything remotely approaching the human and the civilized was better luck than he could have dreamed or prayed for.

Besides, there were sun-stones in this place. He looked hungrily at the head of the circling watcher, and then began to scramble down the broken outer face of the bastion.

The black wings slipped silently after him down the sky.

About a hundred feet above the valley floor he came to an overhang. There was no way past it but to jump. He clung to a bush and let himself down as far as he could, and then dropped some four or five yards to a slope of springy turf. The fall knocked the wind out of him, and as he lay gasping a chill doubt crept into his mind.

He could see the land quite clearly now, the pattern of the fields, the far-off city. Except for the group of riders, nothing stirred. The fields, the plain were empty of men, the little villages still as death.

And he saw, swinging lazily above a belt of trees by the river, a second black-winged shadow, watching.

The trees were not far away. The riders were coming toward them and him. It seemed to Trevor now that the men were perhaps a party of hunters, but there was something alarming about the utter disappearance of all other life. It was as though the gong had been a warning for all to take cover while the hunt was abroad.

The sharp-eyed lizards were the hounds that went before to find and flush the game. Glancing up at the ominous sentinel above his own head, Trevor had a great desire to see what the quarry was that hid in the belt of trees.

There was no way back to the partial security of the lake basin. The overhang cut him off from that. The futility of trying to hide was apparent, but nevertheless he wormed in among some crimson ferns. The city was at his left. To the right, the fertile plain washed out into a badland of lava and shattered rock, which narrowed and vanished around a shoulder of purple basalt. This defile was still in deep shadow.

The riders were still far away. He saw them splash across a ford, toy figures making little bursts of spray.

The watcher above the trees darted suddenly downward. The quarry was breaking cover.

Trevor's suspicions crystallized into an ugly certainty. Horror-struck, he watched the bronzed, half-naked figure of a girl emerge from the brilliant undergrowth and run like an antelope toward the badland.

The flying lizard rose, swooped, and struck.

The girl flung herself aside. She carried a length of sapling bound with great thorns, and she lashed out with it at the black brute, grazed it, and ran on.

SHANNACH: THE LAST

The lizard circled and came at her again from behind.

She turned. There was a moment of vicious confusion, in which the leathery wings enveloped her in a kind of dreadful cloak, and then she was running again, but less swiftly, and Trevor could see the redness of blood on her body.

And again the flying demon came.

The thing was trying to head her, turn her back toward the huntsmen. But she would not be turned. She beat with her club at the lizard, and ran, and fell, and ran again. And Trevor knew that she was beaten. The brute would have the life out of her before she reached the rocks.

Every dictate of prudence told Trevor to stay out of this. Whatever was going on was obviously the custom of the country, and none of his business. All he wanted was to get hold of one of these sun-stones and then find a way out of this valley. That was going to be trouble enough without taking on any more.

But prudence was swept away in the fury that rose in him as he saw the hawk swoop down again, with its claws outspread and hungry for the girl's tormented flesh. He sprang up, shouting to her to fight, to hang on, and went running full speed down the slope toward her.

She turned upon him a face of such wild, fierce beauty as he had never seen, the eyes dark and startled and full of a terrible determination. Then she screamed at him, in his own tongue, "Look out!"

He had forgotten his own nemesis. Black wings, claws, the lash of a scaly tail striking like a whip, and Trevor went down, rolling over and staining the turf red as he rolled.

From far off he heard the voices of the huntsmen, shrill and strident, lifted in a wild halloo.

2

For some reason the assault steadied Trevor. He got to his feet and took the club out of the girl's hands, regretting the gun that was buried under a ton of rock on the other side of the mountains.

"Keep behind me," he said. "Watch my back."

She stared at him strangely, but there was no time for questions. They began to run together toward the badland. It seemed a long way off. The lizards screamed and hissed above them. Trevor hefted the club. It was about the size and weight of a baseball bat. He had once been very good at baseball.

"They're coming," said the girl.

"Lie down flat," he told her, and went on, more slowly. She dropped behind him in the grass, her fingers closing over a fragment of stone. The wide wings whistled down.

Trevor braced himself. He could see the evil eyes, yellow and bright as the golden collars, and the brilliant flash of the sun-stones against the jetty scales of the head. They were attacking together, but at different angles, so that he could not face them both.

He chose the one that was going to reach him first, and waited. He let it get close, very close, diving swiftly with its scarlet tongue forking out of its hissing mouth and its sharp claws spread. Then he swung the club with all his might.

It connected. He felt something break. The creature screamed, and then the force of its dive carried it on into him and he lost his footing in a welter of thrashing wings and floundering body. He fell, and the second lizard was on him.

The girl rose. In three long strides she reached him and flung herself upon the back of the scaly thing that ravaged him. He saw her trying to pin it to the ground, hammering methodically at its head with the stone.

He kicked off the wounded one. He had broken its neck, but it was in no hurry to die. He caught up the club and presently the second brute was dead. Trevor found it quite easy to pick up the sun-stone.

He held it in his hand, a strange, tawny, jewel-like thing, with a scrap of bone still clinging to it. It glinted with inner fires, deep and subtle, and an answering spark of wild excitement was kindled in Trevor from the very touch and feel of it, so that he forgot where he was or what he was doing, forgot everything but the eerie crystal that gleamed against his palm.

It was more than a jewel, more even than wealth, that he held there. It was hope and success and a new life.

He had thrown years away prospecting the bitter Mercurian wastes. This trip had been his last gamble, and it had ended with his ship gone, his quest finished, and nothing to look forward to even if he did get back safely, but to become one of the penniless, aging planet-drifters he'd always pitied.

Now all that was changed. This single stone would let him go back to Earth a winner and not a failure. It would pay off all the dreary, lonesome, hazardous years. It would...

It would do so many things if he could get out of this Godforsaken valley with it! *If!*

The girl had got her breath again. Now she said urgently, "Come! They're getting near!"

Trevor's senses, bemused by the sun-stone, registered only vaguely the external stimuli of sight and sound. The riders had come closer. The beasts they rode were taller and slighter than horses. They were not hoofed, but clawed. They had narrow, vicious-looking heads with spiny crests that stood up erect and arrogant. They came fast, carrying their riders lightly.

The men were still too far away to distinguish features, but even at that distance Trevor sensed something peculiar about their faces, something unnatural. They wore splendid harness, and their half-clad bodies were bronzed, but not nearly so deeply as the girl's.

The girl shook him furiously, stirring him out of his dream. "Do you want to be taken alive? Before, the beasts would have torn us apart, and that is quickly over. But we killed the hawks, don't you understand? Now they will take us alive!"

He did not understand in the least, but her obvious preference for a very nasty death instead of capture made him find reserves of strength he thought he had lost in the underground river. There was also the matter of the sun-stone. If they caught him with it they would want it back.

Clutching the precious thing he turned with the girl and ran.

The lava bed was beginning to catch the sun now. The splintered rock showed through, bleak and ugly. The badland and the defile beyond seemed like an entrance into hell, but it did offer shelter of a sort if they could make it.

The drumming of padded feet behind was loud in his ears. He glanced over his shoulder, once. He could see the faces of the huntsmen now. They were not good faces, in either feature or expression, and he saw the thing about them that he had noticed before, the unnatural thing.

In the center of each forehead, above the eyes, a sun-stone was set into flesh and bone.

First the hawk-lizards, and now these...

Trevor's heart contracted with an icy pang. These men were human, as human as himself, and yet they were not. They were alien and wicked and altogether terrifying, and he began to understand why the girl did not wish to come alive into their hands.

SHANNACH: THE LAST

Fleet, implacable, the crested mounts with their strange riders were sweeping in upon the two who fled. The leader took from about his saddle a curved throwing stick and held it, poised. The sun-stone set in his brow flashed like a third, and evil eye.

The lava and the fangs of rock shimmered in the light. Trevor yearned toward them. The brown girl running before him seemed to shimmer also. It hurt very much to breathe. He thought he could not go any farther. But he did, and when the girl faltered he put his arm around her and steadied her on.

He continued to keep an eye out behind him. He saw the curved stick come hurtling toward him and he managed to let it go by. The others were ready now as they came within range. It seemed to Trevor that they were watching him with a peculiar intensity, as though they had recognized him as a stranger and had almost forgotten the girl in their desire to take him.

His bare feet trod on lava already growing hot under the sun. A spur of basalt reared up and made a shield against the throwing sticks. In a minute or two Trevor and the girl were hidden in a terrain of such broken roughness as the man had seldom seen. It was as though some demoniac giant had whipped the molten lava with a pudding-spoon, cracking mountains with his free hand and tossing in the pieces. He understood now why the girl had waited for daylight to make her break. To attempt this passage in the dark would be suicidal.

He listened nervously for sounds of pursuit. He could not hear any, but he remained uneasy, and when the girl flung herself down to rest, he asked,

"Shouldn't we go farther? They might still come."

She did not answer him at once, beyond a shake of the head. He realized that she was looking at him almost as intently as the riders had. It was the first chance she had had to examine him, and she was making the most of it. She noted the cut of his hair, the stubble of beard, the color and texture of his skin, the rags of his shorts that were all he had to cover him. Very carefully she noted them, and then she said in an odd slow voice, as though she were thinking of something else,

"Mounted, the Korins are afraid of nothing. But afoot, and in here, they are afraid of ambush. It has happened before. They can die, you know, just the same as we do."

Her face, for all its youth, was not the face of a girl. It was a woman who looked at Trevor, a woman who had already learned the happy, the passionate, and the bitter things, who had lived with pain and fear and knew better than to trust anyone but herself.

"You aren't one of us," she said.

"No. I came from beyond the mountains." He could not tell whether she believed him or not. "Who, or what, are the Korins?"

"The lords of Korith," she answered, and began to tear strips from the length of white linen cloth she wore twisted about her waist. "There will be time to talk later. We still have far to go. Here, this will stop the bleeding."

In silence they bound each other's wounds and started off again. If Trevor had not been so unutterably weary, and the way so hard, he would have been angry with the girl. And yet there was nothing really to be angry about except that he sensed she was somehow suspicious of him.

Many times they had to stop and rest. Once he asked her, "Why were they—the Korins—hunting *you?*"

"I was running away. Why were they hunting you?"

"Damned if I know. Accident, perhaps. I happened to be where their hawks were flying."

17

SHANNACH: THE LAST

The girl wore a chain of iron links around her neck, a solid chain with no clasp, too small to be pulled over the head. From it hung a round tag with a word stamped on it. Trevor took the tag in his hand.

"Galt," he read. "Is that your name?"

"My name is Jen. Galt is the Korin I belong to. He led the hunt." She gave Trevor a look of fierce and challenging pride and said, as though she were revealing a secret earldom, "I am a slave."

"How long have you been in the valley, Jen? You and I are the same stock, speaking the same language. Earth stock. How does it happen, a colony of this size that no one ever heard of?"

"It's been nearly three hundred years since the Landing," she answered. "I have been told that for generations my people kept alive the hope that a ship would come from Earth and release them from the Korins. It never came. And, except by ship, there is no way in or out of the valley."

Trevor glanced at her sharply. "I found a way in, all right, and I'm beginning to wish I hadn't. And if there's no way out, where are we going?"

"I don't know myself," said Jen, and rose. "But my man came this way, and others before him."

She went on, and Trevor went with her. There was no place else to go.

The heat was unbearable, and they crept in the shadows of the rocks wherever they could. They suffered from thirst, but there was no water. The shoulder of purple basalt loomed impossibly tall before them, and seemed never to grow nearer.

For most of the day they toiled across the lava bed, and at last, when they had almost forgotten that they had ever dreamed of doing it, they rounded the shoulder and came staggering out of the badland

18

into a narrow canyon that seemed like the scar of some cataclysmic wound in the mountain.

Rock walls, raw and riven, rose out of sight on either side, the twisted strata showing streaks of crimson and white and sullen ochre. A little stream crawled in a stony bed, and not much grew beside it.

Jen and Trevor fell by the stream. And while they were still sprawled on the moist gravel, lapping like dogs at the bitter water, men came quietly from among the rocks and stood above them, holding weapons made of stone.

Trevor got slowly to his feet. There were six of these armed men. Like the girl, they wore loin cloths of white cotton, much frayed, and like her they were burned almost black by a lifetime of exposure to a brutal sun. They were all young, knotted and sinewy from hard labor, their faces grim beyond their years. All bore upon their bodies the scars of talons. And they looked at Trevor with a cold, strange look.

They knew Jen, or most of them did. She called them gladly by name, and demanded, "Hugh. Where is Hugh?"

One of them nodded toward the farther wall. "Up there in the caves. He's all right. Who is this man, Jen?"

She turned to study Trevor.

"I don't know. They were hunting him, too. He came to help me. I couldn't have escaped without him. He killed the hawks. But..." She hesitated, choosing her words carefully. "He says he came from beyond the mountains. He knows of Earth and speaks our tongue. And when he killed the hawks he smashed the skull of one and took the sun-stone."

All six started at that. And the tallest of them, a young man with a face as bleak and craggy as the rocks around them, came toward Trevor.

19

"Why did you take the sun-stone?" he asked. His voice held an ugly edge.

Trevor stared at him. "Why the devil do you suppose? Because it's valuable."

The man held out his hand. "Give it to me."

"The hell I will!" cried Trevor furiously. He backed away, just a little, getting set.

The young man came on, and his face was dark and dangerous.

"Saul, wait!" cried Jen.

Saul didn't wait. He kept right on coming. Trevor let him get close before he swung, and he put every ounce of his strength behind the blow.

The smashing fist took Saul squarely in the belly and sent him backward, doubled up. Trevor stood with hunched shoulders, breathing hard, watching the others with feral eyes.

"What are you?" he snarled. "A bunch of thieves? All right, come on! I got that stone the hard way and I'm going to keep it!"

Big words. A big anger. And a big fear behind them. The men were around him in a ring now. There was no chance of breaking away. Even if he did he was so winded they could pull him down in minutes. The stone weighed heavy in his pocket, heavy as half a lifetime of sweat and hunger and hard work, on the rockpiles of Mercury.

Saul straightened up. His face was still gray, but he bent again and picked up a sharp-pointed implement of rock that he had dropped. Then he moved forward. And the others closed in, at the same time, quite silently.

There was a bitter taste in Trevor's mouth as he waited for them. To get his hands on a sun-stone at last, and then to lose it and probably his life too, to this crowd of savages! It was more than anybody ought to be asked to bear.

"Saul, wait!" cried Jen again, pushing in front of him. "He saved my life! You can't just..."

"He's a Korin. A spy."

"He can't be! There's no stone in his forehead. Not even a scar."

Saul's voice was flat and relentless. "He took a sun-stone. Only a Korin would touch one of the cursed things."

"But he says he's from outside the valley! From Earth, Saul. From *Earth!* Things would be different there."

Jen's insistence on that point had at least halted the men temporarily. And Trevor, looking at Saul's face, had suddenly begun to understand something.

"You think the sun-stones are evil," he said.

Saul gave him a somber glance. "They are. And the one you have is going to be destroyed. Now."

Trevor swallowed the bitter anguish that choked him, and did some fast thinking. If the sun-stones had a superstitious significance in this benighted pocket of Mercury—and he could imagine why they might, with those damned unnatural hawks flying around with the equally unnatural Korins—that put a different light on their attitude.

He knew just by looking at their faces that it was "give them the sun-stone or die." Dying at the hands of a bunch of wild fanatics didn't make sense. Better let them have the stone and gamble on getting it back again later. Or on getting another one. They seemed plentiful enough in the valley!

Sure, let's be sensible about it. Let's hand over a lifetime of hoping to a savage with horny palms, and not worry about it. Let's...Oh, hell.

"Here," he said. "All right. Take it."

It hurt. It hurt like giving up his own heart.

SHANNACH: THE LAST

Saul took it without thanks. He turned and laid it on a flat surface of rock, and began to pound the glinting crystal with the heavy stone he had meant to use on Trevor's head. There was a look on his lined, young, craggy face as though he was killing a living thing—a thing that he feared and hated.

Trevor shivered. He knew that sun-stones were impervious to anything but atomic bombardment. But it made him a little sick, none the less, to see that priceless object being battered by a crude stone club.

"It won't break," he said. "You might as well stop."

Saul flung down his weapon so close to Trevor's bare feet that he leaped back. Then he picked up the sun-stone and hurled it as far as he could across the ravine. Trevor heard it clicking faintly as it fell, in among the rocks and rubble at the foot of the opposite cliff. He strained to mark the spot.

"You idiot!" he said to Saul. "You've thrown away a fortune. The fortune I've spent my life trying to find. What's the matter with you? Don't you have any idea at all what those things are worth?"

Saul ignored him, speaking bleakly to the others. "No man with a sun-stone is to be trusted. I say kill him."

Jen said stubbornly, "No, Saul. I owe him my life."

"But he could be a slave, a traitor, working for the Korins."

"Look at his clothes," said Jen. "Look at his skin. This morning it was white, now it's red. Did you ever see a slave that color? Or a Korin, either. Besides, did you ever see him in the valley before? There aren't as many of us as that."

"We can't take any chances," Saul said. "Not us."

"You can always kill him later. But if he *is* from beyond the mountains, perhaps even from Earth—" She said the word hesitantly, as though she did not quite believe there was such a place. "He might

22

know some of the things we've been made to forget. He might help us. Anyway, the others have a right to their say before you kill him."

Saul shook his head. "I don't like it. But—" He hesitated, scowling thoughtfully. "All right. We'll settle it up in the cave. Let's move." He said to Trevor, "You go in the middle of us. And if you try to signal anyone..."

"Who the devil would I signal to?" retorted Trevor angrily. "Listen, I'm sorry I ever got into your bloody valley."

But he was not sorry. Not quite.

His senses were on the alert to mark every twist and turn of the way they went, the way that would bring him back to the sun-stone. The ravine narrowed and widened and twisted, but there was only one negotiable path, and that was beside the stream bed. This went on for some distance, and then the ravine split on a tremendous cliff of bare rock that tilted up and back as though arrested in the act of falling over. The stream flowed from the left-hand fork. Saul took the other one.

They kept close watch on Trevor as he slipped and clambered and sprawled along with them. The detritus of the primeval cataclysm that had shaped this crack in the mountains lay where it had fallen, growing rougher and more dangerous with every eroding storm and cracking frost.

Above him, on both sides, the mountain tops went up and still up, beyond the shallow atmosphere. Their half-seen summits leaned and quivered like things glimpsed from under water, lit like torches by the naked blaze of the sun. There were ledges, lower down. Trevor saw men crouched upon them, among heaps of piled stones. They shouted, and Saul answered them. In this narrow throat no man could get through alive if they chose to stop him.

SHANNACH: THE LAST

After a while they left the floor of the ravine and climbed a path, partly natural and partly so roughly hewn that it seemed natural. It angled steeply up the cliff-face, and at its end was a narrow hole. Saul led the way through it. In single file the others followed, and Trevor heard Jen's voice echoing in some great hollow space beyond, calling Hugh.

There was a cave inside, a very large cave with dim nooks and crannies around its edges. Shafts of sunlight pierced it here and there from cracks in the cliff-face high above, and far at the back of it, where the floor tipped sharply down, a flame burned. Trevor had seen flames like that before on Mercury, where volcanic gases blowing up through a fissure had ignited from some chance spark. It was impressive, a small bluish column twisting upward into rock-curtained distance and roaring evilly. He could feel the air rush past him as the burning pillar sucked it in.

There were people in the cave. Less than a hundred, Trevor thought, not counting a handful of children and striplings. Less than a third of those were women. They all bore the same unmistakable stamp. Hard as life must be for them in the cave, it had been harder before.

He felt his legs buckling under him with sheer weariness. He stood groggily with his back against the rough cave wall.

A stocky young man with knotted shoulder-muscles and sun-bleached hair was holding Jen in his arms. That would be Hugh. He, and the others, were shouting excitedly, asking and answering questions.

Then, one by one, they caught sight of Trevor. And gradually a silence grew and spread.

"All right," said Saul harshly, looking at Trevor. "Let's get this settled."

"You settle it," said Trevor. "I'm tired." He glared at Saul and the unfriendly staring crowd, and they seemed to rock in his vision. "I'm an Earthman. I didn't want to come into your damned valley, and I've been here a night and a day and haven't slept. I'm going to sleep."

Saul started to speak again but Jen's man, Hugh, came up and stood in front of him.

"He saved Jen's life," Hugh said. "Let him sleep."

He led Trevor away to a place at the side where there were heaps of dried vines and mountain creepers, prickly and full of dust but softer than the cave floor. Trevor managed a few vague words of thanks and was asleep before they were out of his mouth.

Hours, weeks, or perhaps it was only minutes later, a rough persistent shaking brought him to again. Faces bent over him. He saw them through a haze, and the questions they asked penetrated to him slowly, and without much meaning.

"Why did you want the sun-stone?"

"Why wouldn't I want it? I could take it back to Earth and sell it for a fortune."

"What do they do with sun-stones on Earth?"

"Build gadgets, super-electronic, to study things. Wave-lengths too short for anything else to pick up. Thought-waves, even. What do you care?"

"Do they wear sun-stones in their foreheads, on Earth?"

"No..." His voice trailed off, and the voices, or the dream of voices, left him.

It was still daylight when he woke, this time normally. He sat up, feeling stiff and sore but otherwise rested. Jen came to him, smiling, and thrust a chunk of what he recognized as some species of rock-lizard into his hands. He gnawed at it wolfishly while she talked, having discovered that this was not the same day, but the next one, and quite late.

"They have decided," she said, "to let you live."

"I imagine you had a lot to do with that. Thanks."

She shrugged her bare shoulders, with the raw wounds on them where the hawk-lizards had clawed her. She had that exhausted, let-down look that comes after tremendous stress, and her eyes, even while she spoke to Trevor, followed Hugh as he worked at some task around the cave.

"I couldn't have done anything if they hadn't believed your story," she told him. "They questioned you when you were too far gone to lie." He had a very dim memory of that. "They didn't understand your answers but they knew they were true ones. Also they examined your clothes. No cloth like that is woven in the valley. And the things that hold them together—" he knew she meant the zippers "—are unknown to us. So you must have come from beyond the mountains. They want to know exactly how, and if you could get back the same way."

"No," said Trevor, and explained. "Am I free to move around, then—go where I want to?"

She studied him a moment before she spoke. "You're a stranger. You don't belong with us. You could betray us to the Korins just as easily as not."

"Why would I do that? They hunted me, too."

"For sun-stones, perhaps. You're a stranger. They would take you alive. Anyway, be careful. Be very careful what you do." From outside came a cry. "Hawks! Take cover, hawks!"

3

Instantly everyone in the cave fell silent. They watched the places in the cave wall where the sunlight came in, the little cracks in the cliff-face. Trevor thought of the hawk-creatures, and how they would be wheeling and slipping along the ravine, searching.

Outside, the rough rock looked all alike. He thought that in that immensity of erosions and crevices they would have a hard time finding the few tiny chinks that led into the cave. But he watched, too, tense with a feeling of danger.

No sound at all came now from the ravine. In that utter stillness, the frightened whimper of a child came with the sudden loudness of a scream. It was instantly hushed. The shafts of sunlight crept slowly up the walls. Jen seemed not to breathe. Her eyes shone, like an animal's.

A black shadow flickered across one of the sunlight bars-flickered, and then was gone. Trevor's heart turned over. He waited for it to come back, to occlude that shaft of light, to slip in along it and become a wide-winged demon with a sun-stone in its brow. For a whole eternity he waited, but it didn't come back, and then a man crept in through the entry hole and said, "They're gone."

Jen put her head down on her knees. She had begun to tremble all over, very quietly, but with spasmodic violence. Before Trevor could reach her, Hugh had her in his arms, talking to her, soothing her. She began to sob then, and Hugh glanced at Trevor across her shoulders.

"She's had a little too much."

"Yes." Trevor looked at the shafts of sunlight. "Do the hawks come very often?"

"They send them every once in a while hoping to catch us off guard. If they could find the cave they could hunt us out of it, drive us back into the valley. So far they haven't found it."

Jen was quiet now. Hugh stroked her with big awkward hands. "She told you, I guess. About yourself, I mean. You've got to be careful."

"Yes," said Trevor. "She told me." He leaned forward. "Listen, I still don't know how you people got here or what it's all about. After we got away from the Korins, Jen said something about a landing, three hundred years ago. Three hundred Earth years?"

"About that. Some of us have remembered enough to keep track."

"The first Earth colonies were being started on Mercury about then, in two or three of the bigger valleys. Mining colonies. Was this one of them?"

Hugh shook his head. "No. The story is that there was a big ship loaded with people from Earth. That's true, of course, because the ship is still here, what's left of it. And so are we. Some of the people on the ship were settlers and some were convicts."

He pronounced the word with the same hatred and scorn that always accompanied the name "Korin." Trevor said eagerly,

"They used to do that in the early days. Use convict labor in the mines. It made so much trouble they had to stop it. Were the Korins...!"

"They were the convicts. The big ship crashed in the valley but most of the people weren't killed. After the crash the convicts killed the men who were in charge of the ship, and made the settlers obey them. That's how it all started. And that's why we're proud we're slaves—because we're descended from the settlers."

Trevor could see the picture quite clearly now, the more so because it had happened before in one way or another. The emigrant ship bound for one of the colonies, driven off its course by the tremendous magnetic disturbances that still made Mercury a spaceman's nightmare.

They couldn't even have called for help or given their position. The terrible nearness of the Sun made any form of radio communication impossible. And then the convicts had broken free and killed the officers, finding themselves unexpectedly in command of a sort of paradise, with the settlers to serve them.

A fairly safe paradise, too. Mercury has an infinite number of these Twilight valleys, all looking more or less alike from space, half hidden under their shallow blankets of air, and only the few that are both accessible and unmistakable because of their size have permanent colonies. Straight up and down, by spaceship, is the only way in or out of most of them, and unless a ship should land directly on them by sheer chance, the erstwhile prisoners would be safe from discovery.

"But the sun-stones?" asked Trevor, touching his forehead.

"What about the sun-stones and the hawks? They didn't have the use of them when they landed."

"No, they came later." Hugh looked around uneasily. "Look, Trevor, it's a thing we don't talk about much. You can see why, when you think what it's done to us. And it's a thing you shouldn't talk about at all."

"But how did they get them in their heads? And why? Especially, why do they waste them on the hawks?"

Jen glanced at him somberly from the circle of Hugh's arm. "We don't know, exactly. But the hawks are the eyes and ears of the Korins. And from the time they used the first sun-stone we've had no hope of getting free from them."

The thing that had been buried in Trevor's subconscious since last night's questioning came suddenly to the surface.

"Thought-waves, that's it! Sure!" He leaned forward excitedly, and Jen told him frantically to lower his voice. "I'll be damned. They've been experimenting with sun-stones for years on Earth-ever since they were discovered, but the scientists never thought of..."

"Do they have the stones on Earth, too?" asked Jen, with loathing.

"No, no, only the ones that are brought from Mercury. Something about Mercury being so close to the Sun, overdose of solar radiation and the extremes of heat, cold, and pressure while the planet was being made, that formed that particular kind of crystal here. I guess that's why they're called sun-stones."

He shook his head. "So that's how they work it—direct mental communication between the Korins and the hawks, by means of the stones. Simple, too. Set them right in the skull, almost in contact with the brain, and you don't need all the complicated machines and senders and receivers they've been monkeying with in the labs for so long." He shivered. "I'll admit I don't like the idea, though. There's something repulsive about it."

Hugh said bitterly, "When they were only men, and convicts, we might have beaten them some day, even though they had all the weapons. But when they became the Korins—" He indicated the darkling alcoves of the cave. "This is the only freedom we can ever have now."

Looking at Hugh and Jen, Trevor felt a great welling-up of pity, for them, and for all these far-removed children of Earth who were now only hunted slaves to whom this burrow in the rock meant freedom. He thought with pure hatred of the Korins who hunted them, with the uncanny hawks that were their far-ranging eyes and ears and weapons. He wished he could hit them with...

He caught himself up sharply. Letting his sympathies run away with him wasn't going to do anybody any good. The only thing that concerned him was to get hold of that sun-stone again and get out of this devil's pocket. He'd spent half a life hunting for a stone, and he wasn't going to let concern over perfect strangers sidetrack him now.

The first step would be getting away from the cave.

It would have to be at night. No watch was kept then on the ledges, for the hawks did not fly in darkness, and the Korins never moved without the hawks. Most of the people were busy in those brief hours of safety. The women searched for edible moss and lichens. Some of the men brought water from the stream at the canyon fork, and others, with stone clubs and crude spears, hunted the great rock-lizards that slept in the crevices, made sluggish by the cold.

Trevor waited until the fourth night, and then when Saul's water party left, he started casually out of the cave after them.

"I think I'll go down with them," he told Jen and Hugh. "I haven't been down that far since I got here."

There seemed to be no suspicion in them of his purpose. Jen said, "Stay close to the others. It's easy to get lost in the rocks."

He turned and went into the darkness after the water party. He followed them down to the fork, and it was quite easy then to slip aside among the tumbled rock and leave them, working his way slowly and silently downstream.

After several days in the dimness of the cave, he found that the star-shine gave him light enough to move by. It was hard going, even so, and by the time he reached the approximate place where Saul had tried to kill him he was bruised and cut and considerably shaken. But he picked his spot carefully, crossed the stream, and began to search.

The chill deepened. The rocks that had been hot under his hands turned cold, and the frost-rime settled lightly on them, and Trevor shivered and swore and scrambled, fighting the numbness out of his body, praying that none of the loose rubble would fall on him and

31

crush him. He had prospected on Mercury for a long time. Otherwise he would not have lived.

He found it more easily than he could have done by day, without a detector. He saw the cold pale light of it gleaming, down among the dark broken rock where Saul had thrown it.

He picked it up.

He dandled the thing in his palm, touching it with loving finger tips. It had a certain cold repellent beauty, glimmering in the darkness—a freakish by-product of Mercury's birth-pangs, unique in the solar system. Its radioactivity was a type and potency harmless to living tissue, and its wonderful sensitivity had made it possible for physicists to explore at least a little into those unknown regions above the first octave.

In a gesture motivated by pure curiosity he lifted the stone and pressed it tight against the flesh between his brows. Probably it wouldn't work this way. Probably it had to be set deep into the bone...

It worked, oh God, it worked, and something had him, something caught him by the naked brain and would not let him go.

Trevor screamed. The thin small sound was lost in the empty dark, and he tried again, but no sound would come. Something had forbidden him to scream. Something was in there, opening out the leaves of his brain like the pages of a child's book, and it wasn't a hawk, or a Korin. It wasn't anything human or animal that he had ever known before. It was something still and lonely and remote, as alien as the mountain peaks that towered upward to the stars, and as strong, and as utterly without mercy.

Trevor's body became convulsed. Every physical instinct was driving him to run, to escape, and he could not. In his throat now there was a queer wailing whimper. He tried to drop the sun-stone. He was forbidden. Rage began to come on the heels of horror, a blind protest against the indecent invasion of his most private mind. The whimpering rose to a sort of catlike squall, an eerie and quite insane sound in the narrow gorge, and he clawed with his free hand at the one that held the sun-stone, tight against his brows.

He tore it loose.

A wrench that almost cracked his brain in two. A flicker of surprise, just before the contact broke, and then a fading flash of anger, and then nothing.

Trevor fell down. He did not quite lose consciousness, but there was an ugly sickness in him and all his bones had turned to water. It seemed a long time before he could get to his feet again. Then he stood there shaking.

There was something in this accursed valley. There was something or someone who could reach out through the sun-stones and take hold of a man's mind. It did that to the Korins and the hawks, and it had done it for a moment to him, and the horror of that alien grasp upon his brain was still screaming inside him.

"But who—?" he whispered hoarsely. And then he knew that the word was wrong. "*What*—?"

For it was not human, it couldn't be human, whatever had held him there wasn't man or woman, brute or human. It was something else, but what it was he didn't want to know, he only wanted to get out—out—

Trevor found that he had begun to run, bruising his shins against rocks. He got a grip on himself, forcing himself to stand still. His breath was coming in great gasps.

He still had the sun-stone clenched in his sweating palm, and he had an almost irresistible desire to fling the thing away with all his strength. But even in the grip of alien horror a man could not throw away the goal of half a lifetime, and he held it, and hated it.

He told himself that whatever it was that reached through the sun-stones could not use them unless they were against the forehead, close to the brain. The thing couldn't harm him if he kept it away from his head.

A terrible thought renewed Trevor's horror. He thought of the Korins, the men who wore sun-stones set forever in their brows. Were they, always and always, in the icy, alien grip of that which had held him? And these were the masters of Jen's people?

He forced that thought away. He had to forget everything except how to get free of this place.

He started at once, still shaken. He couldn't go far before daylight, and he would have to lie up in the rocks through the day and try to make it to the valley wall the next night.

He was glad when daylight came, the first fires of sunrise kindling the peaks that went above the sky.

It was at that moment that a shadow flickered, and Trevor looked up and saw the hawks.

Many hawks. They had not seen him, they were not heeding the rocks in which he crouched. They were flying straight up the ravine, not circling or searching now but going with a sure purpose-fullness, back the way he had come.

He watched them uneasily. There were more than he had ever seen together before. But they flew on up the ravine without turning, and were gone.

"They weren't looking for me," he thought. "But..."

Trevor should have felt relieved, but he didn't. His uneasiness grew and grew, stemming from an inescapable conclusion.

The hawks were going to the cave. They were heading toward it in an exact line, turning neither to right nor left, and this time they were not in any doubt. They, or whoever or whatever dominated them, knew this time exactly where to find the fugitives.

"But that's impossible," Trevor tried to tell himself. "There's no way they could suddenly learn exactly where the cave is after all this time."

No way?

A thing was forcing its way up into Trevor's anxious thoughts, a realization that he did not want to look at squarely, not at all. But it would not be put down, it would not stop tormenting him, and suddenly he cried out to it, a cry of pain and guilt, "No, it couldn't be! It couldn't be through me they learned!" It fronted him relentlessly, the memory of that awful moment in the canyon when whatever had gripped him through the sun-stone had seemed to be turning over the leaves of his brain like the pages of a book.

The vast and alien mind that had gripped his in that dreadful contact had read his own brain clearly, he knew. And in Trevor's brain and memories it had found the secret of the cave. Trevor groaned in an agony of guilt.

He crawled out of his rock-heap and began to run back up the ravine, following the path the hawks had taken. There might still be time to warn them.

Stumbling, running, he passed the canyon fork. And now from above him in the canyon he heard the sounds he dreaded—the sounds of women screaming and men shouting hoarsely in fury and despair. Farther on, over the rocks, scrambling, slipping, gasping for breath, he came to the cave-mouth and the sight he had dreaded.

The hawks had gone into the cave and driven out the slaves. They had them in the canyon now, and they were trying to herd them together and drive them down toward the lava beds. But the slaves were fighting back.

Dark wings beat and thundered in the narrow gorge between the walls of rock. Claws struck and lashing tails cut like whips. Men struggled and floundered and trampled each other. Some died. Some of the hawks died too. But the people were being forced farther down the canyon under the relentless swooping of the hawks. Then Trevor saw Jen. She was a little way from the others. Hugh was with her. He had shoved her into a protecting hollow and was standing over her with a piece of rock in his hands, trying to beat off a hawk. Hugh was hurt badly. He was not doing well.

Trevor uttered a wild cry that voiced all the futile rage in him, and bounded over a slope toward them.

"Hugh, look out!" he yelled. The hawk had risen, and then had checked and turned, to swoop down straight at Hugh's back.

Hugh swung partly around, but not soon enough. The hawk's claws were in his body, deep. Hugh fell down.

Jen was screaming when Trevor reached them. He didn't stop to snatch up a rock. He threw himself onto the hawk that had welded itself to Hugh's back. There was a horrid slippery thrashing of wings under him, and the scaly neck of the thing was terribly strong between Trevor's hands. But not strong enough. He broke it.

It was too late. When his sight cleared, Jen was staring in a strange wild way at the man and hawk lying tangled together in the dust. When Trevor touched her she fought him a little, not as though she saw him really, not as though she saw anything but Hugh's white ribs sticking out.

"Jen, for God's sake, he's dead." Trevor tried to pull her away. "We've got to get away from here."

There might be a chance. The black hawks were driving the humans down the canyon a little below them now, and if they could make the tumbled rocks below the cliff, there was a chance.

4

He had to drag Jen. Her face had gone utterly blank.

In the next minute he realized that they would never reach the rocks, and that there was no chance, none at all. Back from the winged whirl that was driving the humans, two of the hawks came darting at them.

Trevor swung Jen behind him and hoped fiercely that he could get another neck between his hands before they pulled him down.

The dark shadows flashed down. He could see the sun-stones glittering in their heads. They struck straight at him...

But at the last split second they swerved away.

Trevor waited. They came back again, very fast, but this time it was at Jen they struck, and not at him.

He got her behind him again in time. And once more the hawks checked their strike.

The truth dawned on Trevor. The hawks were deliberately refraining from hurting him.

"Whoever gives them their orders, the Korins or that Other, doesn't want me hurt!"

He caught up Jen in his arms and started to run again toward the rocks.

Instantly the hawks struck at Jen. He could not swing her clear in time. Blood ran from the long claw-marks they left in her smooth, tanned shoulders.

Jen cried out. Trevor hesitated. He tried again for the rocks, and Jen moaned as a swift scaly head snapped at her neck.

So that's it, Trevor thought furiously. I'm not to be hurt, but they can drive me through Jen.

And they could, too. He would never get Jen to the concealment of the rocks alive, with those two wide-winged shadows tearing at her.

He had to go the way they wanted or they would leave her as they had left Hugh.

"All right!" Trevor yelled savagely at the circling demons. "Let her alone! I'll go where you want."

He turned, still carrying Jen, plodding after the other slaves who were being herded down the canyon.

All that day the black hawks drove the humans down the watercourse, around the shoulder of basalt and out onto the naked sun-seared lava bed. Some of them dropped and lay where they were, and no effort of the hawks could move them on again. Much of the time Trevor carried Jen. Part of the time he dragged her. For long vague periods he had no idea what he did.

He was in a daze in which only his hatred still was vivid, when he felt Jen pulled away from him. He struggled, and was held—and he looked up to see a ring of mounted men around him. Korins on their crested beasts, the sun-stones glittering in their brows.

They looked down at Trevor, curious, speculative, hostile, their otherwise undistinguished human faces made strangely evil and other-worldly by the winking stones.

"You come with us to the city," one of them said curtly to Trevor. "That woman goes with the other slaves."

Trevor glared up at him. "Why me, to the city?"

The Korin raised his riding whip threateningly. "Do as you're ordered! Mount!"

Trevor saw that a slave had brought a saddled beast to him and was holding it, not looking either at him or the Korins.

"All right," he said. "I'll go with you."

He mounted and sat waiting, his eyes bright with the hatred that burned in him, bright as blown coals. They formed a circle around him and the leader gave a word. They galloped off toward the distant city.

Trevor must have dozed as he rode, for suddenly it was sunset, and they were approaching the city.

Seeing it as he had before, far off and with nothing to measure it against but the overtopping titan peaks, it had seemed no more than a city built of rock. Now he was close to it. Black shadows lay on it, and on the valley, but half way up the opposite mountain wall the light still blazed, reflected downward on the shallow sky, so that everything seemed to float in some curious dimension between night and day. Trevor stared, shut his eyes, and stared again.

The size was wrong.

He looked quickly at the Korins, with the eerie feeling that he might have shrunk to child-size as he slept. But they had not changed—at least, relative to himself. He turned back to the city, trying to force it into perspective.

It rose up starkly from the level plain. There was no gradual guttering out into suburbs, no softening down to garden villas or rows of cottages. It leaped up like a cliff and began, solemn, massive, squat, and ugly. The buildings were square, set stiffly along a square front. They were not tall. Most of them were only one story high. And yet Trevor felt dwarfed by them, as he had never felt dwarfed by the mightiest of Earth's skyscrapers. It was an unnatural feeling, and one that made him curiously afraid.

There were no walls or gateways, no roads leading in. One minute the beasts padded on the grass of the open plain. The next, their claws were clicking on a stone pave and the buildings closed them in, hulking, graceless, looking sullen and forlorn in the shadowed light. There was no sound in them anywhere, no gleaming of lamps in the black embrasures of cavernous doors. The last furious glare of the hidden sun seeped down from the high peaks and stained their upper walls, and they were old—half as old, Trevor thought, as the peaks themselves.

It was the window embrasures, the doors, and the steps that led up to them that made Trevor understand suddenly what was wrong. And the latent fear that had been in him sprang to full growth. The city, and the buildings in it, the steps and the doors and the height of the windows, were perfectly in proportion, perfectly normal—if the people who lived there were twenty feet high.

He turned to the Korins. "You never built this place. Who built it?"

The one called Galt, who was nearest him, snarled, "Quiet, slave!"

Trevor looked at him, and at the other Korins. Something about their faces and the way they rode along the darkening empty street told him they too were afraid.

He said, "You, the Korins, the lordly demigods who ride about and send your hawks to hunt and slay—you're more afraid of your master than the slaves are of you!"

They turned toward him pallid faces that burned with hatred.

He remembered how that other had gripped his brain back in the canyon. He remembered how it had felt. He understood many things now.

He asked, "How does it feel to be enslaved, Korins? Not just enslaved in body, but in mind and soul?"

Galt turned like a striking snake. But the blow never fell. The upraised hand with the heavy whip suddenly checked, and then sank down again. Only the eyes of the Korin glowed with a baleful helplessness under the winking sun-stone.

Trevor laughed without humor. "It wants me alive. I guess I'm safe, then. I guess I could tell you what I think of you. You're still convicts, aren't you? After three hundred years. No wonder you hate the slaves."

Not the same convicts, of course. The sun-stones didn't give longevity. Trevor knew how the Korins propagated, stealing women from among the slaves, keeping the male children and killing the female. He laughed again.

"It isn't such a good life after all, is it, being a Korin? Even hunting and killing can't take the taste out of your mouths. No wonder you hate the others! They're enslaved, all right, but they're not owned."

They would have liked to kill him but they could not. They were forbidden. Trevor looked at them, in the last pale flicker of the afterglow. The jewels and the splendid harness, the bridles of the beasts heavy with gold, the weapons—they looked foolish now, like the paper crowns and glass beads that children deck themselves with when they pretend to be kings. These were not lords and masters. These were only little men, and slaves. And the sun-stones were a badge of shame.

The cavalcade passed on. Empty streets, empty houses with windows too high for human eyes to look through and steps too tall for human legs to climb. Full dark, and the first stunning crash of thunder, the first blaze of lightning between the cliffs. The mounts were hurrying now, almost galloping to beat the lightning and the scalding rain.

They were in a great square. Around it was a stiff rectangle of houses, and these were lighted with torchlight, and in the monstrous doorways here and there a little figure stood, a Korin, watching.

In the exact center of the square was a flat low structure of stone, having no windows and but a single door.

They reined the beasts before that lightless entrance. "Get down," said Galt to Trevor. A livid reddish flaring in the sky showed Trevor

43

the Korin's face, and it was smiling, as a wolf smiles before the kill. Then the thunder came, the downpour of rain, and he was thrust bodily into the doorway.

He stumbled over worn flagging in the utter dark, but the Korins moved sure-footedly as cats. He knew they had been here many times before, and he knew that they hated it. He could feel the hate and the fear bristling out from the bodies that were close to his, smell them in the close hot air. They didn't want to be here but they had to. They were bidden.

He would have fallen head-foremost down the sudden flight of steps if someone had not caught his arm. They were huge steps. They were forced to go down them as small children do, lowering themselves bodily from tread to tread. A furnace blast of air came up the well, but in spite of the heat Trevor felt cold. He could feel how the hard stone of the stairs had been worn into deep hollows by the passing of feet. Whose feet? And going where?

A sulphurous glow began to creep up through the darkness. They went down what seemed a very long way. The glow brightened, so that Trevor could once more make out the faces of the Korins. The heat was overpowering, but still there was a coldness around Trevor's heart.

The steps ended in a long low hall, so long that the farther end of it was lost in vaporous shadow. Trevor thought that it must have been squared out of a natural cavern, for here and there in the rocky floor small fumaroles burned and bubbled, giving off the murky light and a reek of brimstone.

Along both sides of the hall were rows of statues seated in stone chairs.

Trevor stared at them, with the skin crawling up and down his back. Statues of men and women—or rather, of creatures manlike and womanlike—sitting solemn and naked, their hands folded in their laps, their eyes, fashioned of dull, reddish stone, looking straight ahead, their features even and composed, with a strange sad patience clinging to the stony furrows around mouth and cheek. Statues that would be perhaps twenty feet tall if they were standing, carved by a master's chisel out of a pale substance that looked like alabaster.

Galt caught his arm. "Oh, no, you won't run away. You were laughing, remember? Come on, I want to see you laugh some more."

They forced him along between the rows of statues. Quiet statues, with a curiously ghostly look of thoughtfulness—of thoughts and feelings long vanished but once there, different from those of humans, perhaps, but quite as strong. No two of them were alike, in face or body. Trevor noted among them things seldom seen in statues, a maimed limb, a deformity, or a completely nondescript face that would offer neither beauty nor ugliness for an artist to enlarge upon. Also, they seemed all to be old, though he could not have said why he thought so.

There were other halls opening off this main one. How far they went he had no means of guessing, but he could see that in them were other shadowy rows of seated figures.

Statues. Endless numbers of statues, down here in the darkness underneath the city...

He stopped, bracing himself against his captors, gripping the hot rock with his bare feet.

"This is a catacomb," he said. "Those aren't statues, they're bodies, dead things sitting up,"

"Come on," said Galt. "Come on, and laugh!"

They took him, and there were too many to fight. And Trevor knew that it was not them he had to fight. Something was waiting for him down in that catacomb. It had had his mind once. It would—

SHANNACH: THE LAST

They were approaching the end of the long hall. The sickly light from the fumaroles showed the last of the lines of seated figures-had they died there like that, sitting up, or had they been brought here afterward? The rows on each side ended evenly, the last chairs exactly opposite each other.

But against the blank end wall was a solitary seat of stone, facing down the full gloomy length of the hall, and on it sat a manlike shape of alabaster, very still, the stony hands folded rigidly upon the stony thighs. A figure no different from the others, except....

Except that the eyes were still alive.

The Korins dropped back a little. All but Galt. He stayed beside Trevor, his head bent, his mouth sullen and nervous, not looking up at all. And Trevor stared into the remote and somber eyes that were like two pieces of carnelian in that pale alabaster face, and yet were living, sentient, full of a deep and alien sorrow.

It was very silent in the catacomb. The dreadful eyes studied Trevor, and for just a moment his hatred was tempered by a strange pity as he thought what it must be like for the brain, the intelligence behind those eyes, already entombed, and knowing it.

"A long living and a long dying. The blessing and the curse of my people."

The words were soundless, spoken inside his brain. Trevor started violently. Almost he turned to flee, remembering the torture of that moment in the canyon, and then he found that while he had been staring, a force as gentle and stealthy as the gliding of a shadow had already invaded him. And he was forbidden.

"At this range I do not need the sun-stones," murmured the silent voice within him. "Once I did not need them at all. But I am old."

Trevor stared at the stony thing that watched him, and then he thought of Jen, of Hugh lying dead with a dead hawk in the dust, and the strangeness left him, and his bitter passion flared again.

46

"So you hate me as well as fear me, little human? You would destroy me?" There was a gentle laughter inside Trevor's mind. "I have watched generations of humans die so swiftly. And yet I am here, as I was before they came, waiting."

"You won't be here forever," snarled Trevor. "These others like you died. You will!"

"Yes. But it is a slow dying, little human. Your body chemistry is like that of the plants, the beasts, based upon carbon. Quick to grow. Quick to wither away. Ours was of another sort. We were like the mountains, cousin to them, our body cells built of silicon, even as theirs. And so our flesh endures until it grows slow and stiff with age. But even then we must wait long, very long, for death."

Something of the truth of that long waiting came to Trevor, and he felt a shuddering thankfulness for the frailty of human flesh.

"I am the last," whispered the silent voice. "For a while I had companionship of minds, but the others are all gone before me, long ago."

Trevor had a nightmare vision of Mercury, in some incalculable future eon, a frozen world taking its last plunge into the burned-out sun, bearing with it these endless rows of alabaster shapes, sitting in their chairs of stone, upright in the dead blackness underneath the ice.

He fought back to reality, clutching his hatred as a swimmer clings to a plank, his voice raw with passion and bitterness as he cried out.

"Yes, I'll destroy you if I can! What else could you expect after what you've done?"

"Oh, no, little human, you will not destroy me. You will help me."

Trevor glared. "Help you? Not if you kill me!"

"There will be no killing. You would be of no use to me dead. But alive you can serve me. That is why you were spared."

"Serve you—like *them*?" He swung to point to the waiting Korins, but the Korins were not waiting now, they were closing in on him, their hands reaching for him.

Trevor struck out at them. He had a fleeting thought of how weird this battle of his with the Korins must look, as they struck and staggered on the stone paving beneath the looming, watching thing of stone.

But even as he had that thought, the moment of struggle ended. An imperious command hit his brain, and black oblivion closed down upon him like the sudden clenching of a fist.

5

Darkness. He was lost in it, and he was not himself any more. He fled through the darkness, groping, crying out for something that was gone. And a voice answered him, a voice that he did not want to hear....

Darkness. Dreams.

Dawn, high on the blazing mountains. He stood in the city, watching the light grow bright and pitiless, watching it burn on the upper walls and then slip downward into the streets, casting heavy shadows in the openings of door and window, so that the houses looked like skulls with empty eyeholes and gaping mouths. The buildings no longer seemed too big. He walked between them, and when he came to steps he climbed them easily, and the window ledges were no higher than his head. He knew these buildings. He looked at each one as he passed, naming it, remembering with a long, long memory.

The hawks came down to him, the faithful servants with the sun-stones in their brows. He stroked their pliant necks, and they hissed softly with pleasure, but their shallow minds were empty of everything but that vague sensation. He passed on through the familiar streets, and in them nothing stirred. All through the day from dawn to sunset, and in the darkness that came afterward, nothing stirred, and there was a silence among the stones.

He could not endure the city. His time was not yet, though the first subtle signs of age had touched him. But he went down into the catacombs and took his place with those others who were waiting and could still speak to him with their minds, so that he should not be quite alone with the silence.

The years went by, leaving no traces of themselves in the unchanging gloom of the mortuary halls.

SHANNACH: THE LAST

One by one those last few minds were stilled until all were gone. And by that time age had chained him where he was, unable to rise and go again into the city where he had been young, the youngest of all...Shannach, they had named him—The Last.

So he waited, alone. And only one who was kin to the mountains could have borne that waiting in the place of the dead.

Then, in a burst of flame and thunder, new life came into the valley. Human life. Soft, frail, receptive life, intelligent, unprotected, possessed of violent and bewildering passions. Very carefully, taking its time, the mind of Shannach reached out and gathered them in.

Some of the men were more violent than the others. Shannach saw their emotions in patterns of scarlet against the dark of his inner mind. They had already made themselves masters, and a number of these frail sensitive brains had snapped out swiftly because of them. "These I will take for my own," thought Shannach. "Their mind-patterns are crude, but strong, and I am interested in death."

There had been a surgeon aboard the ship but he was dead. However, there was no need of a surgeon for what was about to be done. When Shannach had finished talking to the men he had chosen, telling them of the sun-stones, telling them the truth, but not all of it—when those men had eagerly agreed to the promise of power—Shannach took complete control. And the clumsy convict hands that moved now with such exquisite skill were as much his instruments as the scalpels of the dead surgeon that they wielded, making the round incision and the delicate cutting of the bone.

Who was the man that lay there, quiet under the knife? Who were the ones that bent above him, with the strange stones in their brows? Names. There are names and I know them. Closer, closer. I know that man who lies there with blood between his eyes...

Trevor screamed. Someone slapped him across the face, viciously and with intent. He screamed again, fighting, clawing, still blinded by the visions and the dark mists, and that voice that he dreaded so much spoke gently in his mind, "It's all over, Trevor. It is done."

The hard hand slapped him again, and a rough human voice said harshly, "Wake up. Wake up, damn it!"

He woke. He was in the middle of a vast room, crouched down in the attitude of a fighter, shivering, sweating, his hands outstretched and grasping nothing. He must have sprung there, half unconscious, from the tumbled pallet of skins against the wall. Galt was watching him.

"Welcome, Earthman. How does it feel to be one of the masters?"

Trevor stared at him. A burning flood of light fell in through the tall windows so high above his head, setting the sun-stone ablaze between the Korin's sullen brows. Trevor's gaze fixed on that single point of brilliance.

"Oh, yes," said Galt. "It's true."

It struck Trevor with an ugly shock that Galt's lips had not moved, and that he had made no audible sound.

"The stones give us a limited ability," Galt went on, still without speaking aloud. "Not like His, of course. But we can control the hawks, and exchange ideas between us when we want to if the range isn't too far. Naturally, our minds are open to Him any time he wants to pry."

"There's no pain," Trevor whispered, desperately trying to make the thing not be so. "My head doesn't ache."

"Of course not. He takes care of that."

Shannach? If it isn't so, how do I know that name? And that dream, that endless nightmare in the catacombs.

Galt winced. "We don't use that name. He doesn't like it." He looked at Trevor. "What's the matter, Earthman? Why so green? You were laughing once, remember? Where's your sense of humor now?"

He caught Trevor abruptly by the shoulders and turned him around so that he faced a great sheet of polished glassy substance set into the wall. A mirror for giants, reflecting the whole huge room, reflecting the small dwarfed figures of the men.

"Go on," said Galt, pushing Trevor ahead of him. "Take a look."

Trevor shook off the Korin's grasp. He moved forward by himself, close to the mirror. He set his hands against the chill surface and stared at what he saw there. And it was true.

Between his brows a sun-stone winked and glittered. And his face, the familiar, normal, not-too-bad face he had been used to all his life, was transformed into something monstrous and unnatural, a goblin mask with a third, and evil eye.

A coldness crept into his heart and bones. He backed away a little from the mirror, his hands moving blindly upward, slowly toward the stone that glistened between his brows. His mouth was twisted like a child's, and two tears rolled down his cheeks.

His fingers touched the stone. And then the anger came. He sank his nails into his forehead, clawing at the hard stone, not caring if he died after he had torn it out.

Galt watched him. His lips smiled but his eyes were hateful.

Blood ran down the sides of Trevor's nose. The sun-stone was still there. He moaned and thrust his nails in deeper, and Shannach let him go until he had produced one stab of agony that cut his head in two and nearly dropped him. Then Shannach sent in the full force of his mind. Not in anger, for he felt none, and not in cruelty, for he was no more cruel than the mountain he was kin to, but simply because it was necessary.

Trevor felt that cold and lonely power roll down on him like an avalanche. He braced himself to meet it, but it broke his defenses, crushed them, made them nothing, and moved onward against the inmost citadel of his mind.

In that reeling, darkened fortress all that was wholly Trevor crouched and clung to its armament of rage, remembering dimly that once, in a narrow canyon, it had driven back this enemy and broken free. And then some crude animal instinct far below the level of conscious thought warned him not to press the battle now, to bury his small weapon and wait, letting his last redoubt of which he was yet master go untouched and perhaps unnoticed by his captor.

Trevor let his hands drop limply and his mind go slack. The cold black tide of power paused, and then he felt it slide away, withdrawing from those threatened walls. Out of the edges of it, Shannach spoke.

"Your mind is tougher than these valley-bred Korins. They're well conditioned, but you—you remember that you defied me once. The contact was imperfect then. It is not imperfect now. Remember that, too, Trevor."

Trevor drew in a long, unsteady breath. He whispered, "What do you want of me?"

"Go and see the ship. Your mind tells me that it understands these things. See if it can be made to fly again."

That order took Trevor completely by surprise. "The ship! But why...?"

Shannach was not used to having his wishes questioned, but he answered patiently, "I have still a while to live. Several of your short generations. I have had too much of this valley, too much of these catacombs. I want to leave them."

Trevor could understand that. Having had that nightmare glimpse into Shannach's mind, he could perfectly understand. For one brief moment he was torn with pity for this trapped creature who was alone in the universe. And then he wondered, "What would you do if you could leave the valley? What would you do to another settlement of men?"

"Who knows? I have one thing left to me—curiosity."

"You'd take the Korins with you, and the hawks?"

"Some. They are my eyes and ears, my hands and feet. But you object, Trevor."

"What difference does that make?" said Trevor bitterly. "I'll go look at the ship."

"Come on," said Galt, taking up an armful of torches. "I'll show you the way."

They went out through the tall door into the streets between the huge square empty houses. The streets and houses that Trevor had known in his dream, remembering when there were lights and voices in them. Trevor noticed only that Galt was leading him out on the opposite side of the city, toward the part of the valley he had never visited. And then his mind reverted to something that not even the shock of his awakening could drive out of his consciousness. Jen.

A sudden panic sprang up in him. How long had it been since the darkness fell on him there in the catacomb? Long enough for almost anything to happen. He envisioned Jen being torn by hawks, of her body lying dead as Hugh's had lain, and he started to reach out for Galt, who had owned them both. But abruptly Shannach spoke to him, in that eerie silent way he was getting used to. "The woman is safe. Here, look for yourself."

His mind was taken firmly and directed into a channel completely new to him. He felt a curious small shock of contact, and suddenly he was looking down from a point somewhere in the sky at a walled paddock with a number of tiny figures in it. His own eyes would have seen them as just that, but the eyes he was using now were keen as an eagle's, though they saw no color but only black and white and the shadings in between. So he recognized one of the distant figures as Jen.

He wanted to get closer to her, much closer, and rather sulkily his point of vision began to circle down dropping lower and lower. Jen looked up. He saw the shadow of wide wings sweep across her and realized that of course he was using one of the hawks. He pulled it back so as not to frighten her, but not before he had seen her face. The frozen stoniness was gone, and in its place had come the look of a wounded tigress.

"I want her," Trevor said to Shannach.

"She belongs to Galt. I do not interfere."

Galt shrugged. "You're welcome. But keep her chained. She's too dangerous now for anything but hawk-meat."

The ship was not far beyond the city. It lay canted over on its side, just clear of a low spur jutting out from the barrier cliff. It had hit hard, and some of the main plates were buckled, but from the outside the damage did not seem irreparable, if you had the knowledge and the tools to work with. Three hundred years ago it might have been made to fly again, only those who had the knowledge and the will were dead. And the convicts wanted to stay where they were.

The tough metal of the outer skin, alloyed to resist friction that could burn up a meteor, had stood up pretty well under three centuries of Mercurian climate. It was corroded, and where the breaks were the inner shells were eaten through with rust, but the hulk still retained the semblance of a ship.

"Will it fly?" asked Shannach eagerly.

"I don't know yet," Trevor answered.

Galt lighted a torch and gave it to him. "I'll stay out here."

Trevor laughed. "How are you ever going to fly over the mountains?"

"He'll see to that when the time comes," Galt muttered. "Take the rest of these torches. It's dark in there."

Trevor climbed in through the gaping lock, moving with great caution on the tilted, rust-red decks. Inside, the ship was a shambles. Everything had been stripped out of it that could be used, leaving only bare cubicles with the enamel peeling off the walls and a moldering litter of junk.

In a locker forward of the air lock he found a number of space-suits. The fabric was rotted away, but a few of the helmets were still good and some half score of the oxygen bottles had survived, the gas still in them.

Shannach urged him on impatiently. "Get to the essentials, Trevor!"

The bridge room was still intact, though the multiple thickness of glassite in the big ports showed patterns of spidery cracks. Trevor examined the controls. He was strictly a planetary spacer, used to flying his small craft within spitting distance of the world he was prospecting, and there were a few gadgets here he didn't understand, but he could figure the board well enough.

"Not far, Trevor. Only over the mountains. I know from your mind—and I remember from the minds of those who died after the landing—that beyond the mountain wall there is a plain of dead rock, more than a hundred of your reckoning in miles, and then another ridge that seems solid but is not, and beyond that pass there is a fertile valley twenty times bigger than Korith, where Earthmen live."

"Only partly fertile, and the mines that brought the Earthmen are pretty well worked out. But a few ships still land there, and a few Earthmen still hang on."

"That is best. A small place, to begin…"

"To begin what?"

"Who can tell? You don't understand, Trevor. For centuries I have known exactly what I would do. There is a kind of rebirth in not knowing."

Trevor shivered and went back to studying the controls. The wiring, protected by layers of imperviplast insulation and conduit, seemed to be in fair shape. The generator room below had been knocked about, but not too badly. There were spare batteries. Corroded, yes, but if they were charged, they could hold for a while.

"Will it fly?"

"I told you I don't know yet. It would take a lot of work."

"There are many slaves to do this work."

"Yes. But without fuel it's all useless."

"See if there is fuel."

The outlines of that hidden thing in Trevor's secret mind were coming clearer now. He didn't want to see them out in the full light where Shannach could see them too. He thought hard about generators, batteries, and the hooking up of leads.

He crept among the dark bowels of the dead ship, working toward the stern. The torch made a red and smoky glare that lit up deserted wardrooms and plundered holds. One large compartment had a heavy barred and bolted door that had bent like tin in the crash. "That's where they came from," Trevor thought, "like wolves out of a trap."

In the lower holds that had taken the worst of the impact were quantifies of mining equipment and farm machinery, all smashed beyond use but formidable looking none the less, with rusty blades and teeth and queer hulking shapes. They made him think of weapons, and he let the thought grow, adorning it with pictures of men going down under whirring reapers. Shannach caught it.

"Weapons?"

"They could be used as such. But the metal in them would repair the hull."

He found the fuel bunkers. The main supply was used to the last grain of fissionable dust, but the emergency bunkers still showed some content on the mechanical gauges. Not much, but enough.

6

A hard excitement began to stir in Trevor, too big to be hidden in that secret corner of his mind. He didn't try. He let it loose, and Shannach murmured.

"You are pleased. The ship will fly, and you are thinking that when you reach that other valley and are among your own people again, you will find means to destroy me. Perhaps, but we shall see."

In the smoky torchlight, looking down from a sagging catwalk above the firing chambers and the rusty sealed-in tubes, Trevor smiled. A lie could be thought as well as spoken. And Shannach, in a manner of speaking, was only human.

"I'll need help. All the help there is."

"You'll have it."

"It'll take time. Don't hurry me and don't distract me. Remember, I want to get over the mountains as bad as you do."

Shannach laughed.

Trevor got more torches and went to work in the generator room. He felt that Shannach had withdrawn from him, occupied now with rounding up the Korins and the slaves. But he did not relax his caution. The open areas of his mind were filled with thoughts of vengeance to come when he reached that other valley.

Gradually the exigencies of wrestling with antiquated and partly ruined machinery drove everything else away. That day passed, and a night, and half another day before all the leads were hooked the way he wanted them, before one creaky generator was operating on one-quarter normal output, and the best of the spare batteries were charging.

He emerged from the torchlit obscurity into the bridge, blinking mole-like in the light, and found Galt sitting there.

"He trusts you," the Korin said, "but not too far."

SHANNACH: THE LAST

Trevor scowled at him. Exhaustion, excitement, and a feeling of fate had combined to put him into an unreal state where his mind operated more or less independently. A hard protective shell had formed around that last little inner fortress so that it was hidden even from himself, and he had come almost to believe that he was going to fly this ship to another valley and battle Shannach there. So he was not surprised to hear Shannach say softly in his mind,

"You might try to go away alone. I wouldn't want that, Trevor."

Trevor grunted. "I thought you controlled me so well I couldn't spit if you forbade it."

"I am dealing with much here that I don't comprehend. We were never a mechanical people. Therefore some of your thoughts, while I read them clearly, have no real meaning for me. I can handle you, Trevor, but I'm taking no chances with the ship."

"Don't worry," Trevor told him. "I can't possibly take the ship up before the hull's repaired. It would fall apart on me." That was true, and he spoke it honestly.

"Nevertheless," said Shannach, "Galt will be there, as my hands and feet, an extra guard over that object which you call a control-bank, and which your mind tells me is the key to the ship. You are forbidden to touch it until it is time to go."

Trevor heard Shannach's silent laughter.

"Treachery is implicit in your mind, Trevor. But I'll have time. Impulses come swiftly and cannot be read beforehand. But there is an interval between the impulse and the realization of it. Only a fraction of a second, perhaps, but I'll have time to stop you."

Trevor did not argue. He was shaking a little with the effort of not giving up his last pitiful individuality, of fixing his thoughts firmly on the next step toward what Shannach wanted and looking neither to the right nor to the left of it. He ran a grimy hand over his face, shrinking from the touch of the alien disfigurement in his forehead, and said sullenly,

"The holds have to be cleared. The ship won't lift that weight any more, and we need the metal for repairs." He thought again strongly of weapons. "Send the slaves."

"No," said Shannach firmly. "The Korins will do that. We won't put any potential weapons in the hands of the slaves."

Trevor allowed a wave of disappointment to cross his mind, and then he shrugged. "All right. But get them at it."

He went and stood by the wide ports looking out over the plain toward the city. The slaves were gathered at a safe distance from the ship, waiting like a herd of cattle until they should be needed. Some mounted Korins guarded them while the hawks wheeled overhead.

Coming toward the ship, moving with a resentful slowness, was a little army of Korins. Trevor could sense the group thought quite clearly. In all their lives they had never soiled their hands with labor, and they were angry that they had now to do the work of slaves.

Digging his nails into his palms, Trevor went aft to show them what to do. He couldn't keep it hidden much longer, this thing that he had so painfully concealed under layers of half-truths and deceptions. It had to come out soon, and Shannach would know.

In the smoky glare of many torches the Korins began to struggle with the rusting masses of machinery in the after holds.

"Send more down here," Trevor said to Shannach. "These things are heavy."

"They're all there now except those that guard the slaves. They cannot leave."

"All right," said Trevor. "Make them work."

He went back up along the canting decks, along the tilted passages, moving slowly at first, then swifter, swifter, his bare feet scraping on the flakes of rust, his face, with the third uncanny eye, gone white and strangely set. His mind was throwing off muddy streams of thought, confused and meaningless, desperate camouflage to hide until the last second what was underneath.

"Trevor!"

That was Shannach, alert, alarmed.

It was coming now, the purpose, out into the light. It had to come, it could not be hidden any longer. It burst up from its secret place, one strong red flare against the darkness, and Shannach saw it, and sent the full cold power of his mind to drown it out.

Trevor came into the bridge room, running.

The first black wave of power hit him, crushed him. The bridge room lengthened out into some weird dimension of delirium, with Galt waiting at the far end. Behind Galt the one small, little key that needed to be touched just once.

The towering might of Shannach beat him back, forbidding him to think, to move, to be. But down in that beleaguered part of Trevor's mind the walls still held, with the bright brand of determination burning in them.

This was the moment, the time to fight. And he dug up that armament of fury he had buried there. He let it free, shouting at the alien force, "I beat you once! I beat you!"

The deck swam under his feet. The peeling bulkheads wavered past like veils of mist. He didn't know whether he was moving or not, but he kept on while the enormous weight bore down on his quivering brain, a mountain tilting, falling, seeking to smother out the fury that was all he had to fight with.

Fury for himself, defiled and outraged. Fury for Jen, with the red scars on her shoulders. Fury for Hugh lying dead under an obscene killer, fury for all the generations of decent people who had lived and died in slavery so that Shannach's time of waiting might be lightened.

He saw Galt's face, curiously huge, close to his own. It was stricken and amazed. Trevor's bared teeth glistened.

"I beat him once," he said to the Korin.

Galt's hands were raised. There was a knife in his girdle, but he had been bidden not to use it, not to kill. Only Trevor could make the ship to fly. Galt reached out and took him but there was an un-sureness in his grip, and his mind was crying out to Shannach, "You could not make him stop! You could not!"

Trevor, who was partly merged with Shannach now, heard that cry and laughed. Something in him had burst wide open at Galt's physical touch. He had no control now, no sane thought left, but only a wild intense desire to do two things, one of which was to destroy this monster that had hold of him.

"Kill him," said Shannach suddenly. "He's mad, and no one can control an insane human."

Galt did his best to obey. But Trevor's hands were already around the Korin's throat, the fingers sinking deep into the flesh. There was a sharp snapping of bone.

He dropped the body. He could see nothing now except one tiny point of light in a reeling darkness. That single point of light had a red key in the center of it. Trevor reached out and pushed it down. That was the other thing.

For a short second nothing happened. Trevor sagged down across Galt's body. Shannach was somewhere else, crying warnings that came too late. Trevor had time to draw one harsh triumphant breath and brace himself.

The ship leaped under him. There was a dull roar, and then another, as the last fuel bunkers let go. The whole bridge room rolled and came to rest with a jarring shock that split the ports wide open, and the world was full of the shriek and crash of metal being torn and twisted and rent apart. Then it quieted. The ground stopped shaking and the deck settled under Trevor. There was silence.

Trevor crawled up the new slope of the bridge room floor, to the shattered lock and through it, into the pitiless sunlight. He could see now exactly what he had done. And it was good. It had worked. That last small measure of fuel had been enough.

The whole after part of the hulk was gone, and with it had gone all but a few of Shannach's Korins, trapped in the lower holds.

And then, in pure surprise, Shannach spoke inside Trevor's mind. "I grow old indeed! I misjudged the toughness and the secrecy of a fresh, strong mind. I was too used to my obedient Korins."

"Do you see what's happening to the last of them?" Trevor asked savagely. "Can you see?"

The last of the Korins who had been outside with the slaves seemed to have been stunned and bewildered by the collapse of their world. And with the spontaneity of a whirlwind, the slaves had risen against this last remnant of their hated masters. They had waited for a long, long time, and now the Korins and the hawks were being done to death.

"Can you see it, Shannach?"

"I can see, Trevor. And—they're coming now for you!"

They were. They were coming, blood-mad against all who wore the sun-stone, and Jen was in the forefront of them, and Saul, whose hands were red.

Trevor knew that he had less than a half-minute to speak for his life. And he was aware that Shannach, still withdrawn, watched now with an edged amusement.

Trevor said harshly to Saul and all of them, "So I give you your freedom, and you want to kill me for it?"

Saul snarled, "You betrayed us in the cave, and now..."

"I betrayed you, but without intent. There was someone stronger than the Korins, that even you didn't know about. So how should I have known?"

Trevor talked fast, then, talking for his life, telling them about Shannach and how the Korins themselves were enslaved.

"A lie," spat Saul.

"Look for yourselves in the crypts underneath the city! But be careful."

He looked at Jen, not at Saul. After a moment Jen said slowly, "Perhaps there is a Shannach. Perhaps that's why we were never allowed in the city, so the Korins could go on pretending that they were gods."

"It's another of his lies, I tell you!"

Jen turned to him. "Go and look, Saul. We'll watch him."

Saul hesitated. Finally, he and a half-dozen others went off toward the city.

Trevor sat down on the hot, scorched grass. He was very tired, and he didn't like at all the way the withdrawn shadow of Shannach hovered just outside his mind.

The mountains leaned away from the Sun, and the shadows crawled up the lower slopes. Then Saul and the others returned.

Trevor looked up at their faces and laughed without mirth. "It's true, isn't it?"

"Yes," said Saul, and shivered. "Yes..."

"Did he speak to you?"

"He started to. But—we ran."

SHANNACH: THE LAST

And Saul suddenly cried, out of the depths of fear this time and not of hate, "We can never kill him. It's his valley. And oh God, we're trapped in here with him, we can't get out."

"We can get out," said Trevor.

7

Saul stared at him sickly. "There's no way over the mountains. There isn't even air up there."

"There's a way. I found it in the ship."

Trevor stood up, speaking with a sudden harshness. "Not a way for us all, not now, but if three or four of us go, one may live to make it. And he could bring back men with ships for the others."

He looked at Saul. "Will you try it with me?"

The gaunt man said hoarsely, "I still don't trust you, Trevor! But anything—anything, to get away from that..."

"I'll go too," Jen said suddenly. "I'm as strong as Saul."

That was true, and Trevor knew it. He stared at her for a long minute, but he could not read her face.

Saul shrugged. "All right."

"But it's all craziness," murmured a voice. "You can't breathe up there on the ridges. There's no air!"

Trevor climbed painfully into what was left of the twisted wreck, and brought out the helmets and oxygen bottles that had survived for just this purpose.

"We'll breathe," he said. "These-" He tried for a word that would explain to them, "—these containers hold an essence of air. We can take them with us and breathe."

"But the cold?"

"You have tanned skins, haven't you? And gums? I can show you how to make us protective garments. Unless you'd rather stay here with Shannach."

Saul shivered a little. "No, we'll try it."

In all the hours that followed—while the women of the slaves worked with soft tanned skins and resinous gums, while Trevor labored over the clumsy helmets they must have—in all that time, Shannach was silent.

Silent, but not gone. Trevor felt that shadow on his mind, he knew that Shannach was watching. Yet the Last One made no attempt upon him.

The slaves watched him, too. He saw the fear and hatred still in their eyes as they looked at the sun-stone between his brows.

And Jen watched him, and said nothing, and he could read nothing at all in her face. Was she thinking of Hugh and how the hawks had come?

By mid-afternoon they were ready. They started climbing slowly, toward the passes that went up beyond the sky. He and Saul and Jen were three grotesque and shapeless figures, in the three-layered garments of skin that were crudely sealed with gum, and the clumsy helmets that were padded out with cloth because there was no collar-rest to hold them. Their faces were wrapped close, and they held the ends of the oxygen tubes in their mouths because no amount of ingenuity could make the helmets space-tight.

The evening shadow flowed upward from the valley floor as they climbed, and the men who had come to help them dropped back. These three went on, with Saul leading the way and Trevor last.

And still Shannach had not spoken.

The atmosphere slipped behind them. They were climbing into space now, tiny creatures clambering up an infinity of virgin rock, in the utter black between the blazing peaks above and the flaring lightning's of the evening storm below.

Up and up toward the pass, toiling forward painfully with each other's help where no man could have made it alone, through a numbing and awful cold and silence. Three clumsy, dragging figures, up here above the sky itself, walking in the awfulness of infinity, where the rocks their feet dislodged rushed away as noiseless as a dream, where there was no sound, no light, no time.

Trevor knew they must have reached the pass, for on both sides now there rose up slopes that had never been touched by wind or rain or living root. He staggered on, and presently the ground began to drop and the way was easier. They had passed the crest. And the oxygen was almost gone.

Downward now, stumbling, slipping, sliding, yearning toward the air below. And they were on the other side of the mountain, above the plain of rock that led to...

And then, at last, Shannach—laughed.

"Clever," he said. "Oh, very clever, to escape without a ship! But you will come back, with a ship, and you will take me to the outside world. And I will reward you greatly."

"No," said Trevor, in his mind. "No, Shannach. If we make it, the sun-stone comes out, and we'll come back for the slaves, not for you!"

"No, Trevor." The gentle finality of that denial was coldly frightening. "You are mine now. You surprised and tricked me once, but I know the trick now. Your whole mind is open to me. You cannot withstand me ever again."

It was cold, cold in the darkness below the pass, and the chill went deep into Trevor's soul and froze it.

Saul and Jen were below him now, stumbling down along the rock-strewn lip of a chasm, into the thin high reaches of the air, into sound and life again. He saw them tear away their helmets. He followed them, pulling off his own, gasping the frigid breath into his starved lungs. Shannach said softly,

"We do not need them any longer. They would be a danger when you reach other men. Dispose of them, Trevor."

69

SHANNACH: THE LAST

Trevor started a raging refusal, and then his mind was gripped as by a great hand, shaken and turned and changed. And his fury flowed away into blankness.

But of course, he thought. *There are many boulders, and I can topple them into the chasm so easily...*

He started toward a jagged stone mass, one that would quite neatly brush the two clumsy figures below him into the abyss.

"That is the way, Trevor! But quickly—!"

Trevor knew that Shannach had spoken truth, and that this time he was conquered.

"No, I won't!" he cried to himself, but it was only a weak echo from a fading will-power, a dying self.

"You will, Trevor! And now! They suspect."

Saul and Jen had turned. Trevor's face, open now to the numbing cold which he could scarcely feel, must have told them everything. They started scrambling back up toward him. Only a short distance, but they would be too late.

Trevor shrieked thinly, "Look out—Shannach...!"

He had his hands on it now, on the boulder he must roll to crush them.

But there was another way! He was Shannach's while he lived, but there was a way to avoid again betraying Jen's people, and that way was to live no longer.

He used the last of his dying will to pitch himself toward the brink of the chasm. Hundreds of feet below a man could lie quiet on the rocks through all eternity.

"Trevor, no! No!"

Shannach's powerful command halted him as he swayed on the very edge. And then Jen's arms caught him from behind.

He heard Saul's voice crying, thin and harsh in that upper air, "Push him over! He's a Korin. You saw his face!"

Jen answered, "No! He tried to kill himself for us!"

"But Shannach has him!" Saul cried out.

Shannach had him, indeed, stamping down that final flicker of Trevor's revolt, fiercely commanding him.

"Slay the woman and the man!"

Trevor tried to. He was all Shannach's now. He tried earnestly and with all his strength to kill them, but both the woman and the man had hold of him now. They were too strong for him, and he could not obey the Last One as he wanted to.

"Tie his arms!" Jen was shouting. "We can take him, and he can't do us any harm!"

The anger of Shannach flooded through Trevor, and he raged and struggled, and it was useless. Strips of hide secured his arms and they were dragging him on down out of the mountains, and he could not obey. He could not!

And then he felt the anger of Shannach ebb away into a terrible hopelessness. Trevor felt his own consciousness going, and he went into the darkness bearing in his mind the echo of that last bitter cry,

"I am old—too old..."

8

Trevor awakened slowly, rising above the dark sea of oblivion only to sink again, conscious in those brief intervals that he lay in a bed and that his head ached.

There came a time when he rose, not to sink again. After a while his eyes opened, and he saw a metal ceiling.

"We made it," he said.

"Yes, you made it," said a friendly voice. "This is Solar City. You've been here quite a while."

Trevor turned his head to the voice, to the white-jacketed doctor beside his bed. But he didn't see the man or the room. Not at first. He saw only, upon the bedside table in a tray, a tawny eye that winked and glittered at him.

A sun-stone.

His hand started to rise weakly to his face. The doctor forestalled him.

"Don't bother. It's out. And a delicate job getting it out, it was. You'll have a headache for a while, but anyone would take a headache for a sun-stone!"

Trevor didn't answer that. He said suddenly, "Jen—and Saul...?"

"They're here. Pretty odd folk they are, too. Won't talk to any of us. You're all a blazing mystery, you know."

He went away. When he came back, Jen and Saul were with him. They wore modern synthecloth garments now. Jen looked as incongruous in hers as a leopardess in a silk dress.

She saw the smile in his eyes and cried, "Don't laugh at me—ever!"

It occurred to Trevor that civilizing her would take a long time. He doubted if it would ever be done. And he was glad of that.

She stood looking gravely down at him and then said, "They say you can get up tomorrow."

"That's good," said Trevor.

"You'll have to be careful for a while."

"Yes. I'll be careful."

They said no more than that, but in her steady, grave gaze Trevor read that Hugh and the hawks were forgiven, not forgotten but forgiven, that they two had touched each other and would not let go again.

Saul cried anxiously, "Days we've waited! When can we go back to the valley with a ship for the others?"

Trevor turned to the curiously watching doctor. "Can I charter a ship here?"

"A man with a sun-stone can get almost anything he wants, Trevor! I'll see about it."

The chartered ship that took them back to the valley had a minimum crew, and two mining technicians Trevor had hired. They set down outside the ancient city, and the slaves came surging toward them, half in eagerness, half in awe of this embodiment of misty legend.

Trevor had told Saul what to do. Out up the valley, in the skulls of slain Korins, were sun-stones worth many fortunes. They were going out with the slaves.

"But they're evil—evil!" Saul had cried.

"Not in the outside worlds," Trevor told him. "You people are going to need a start somewhere."

When that was done, when they were all in the ship, Trevor nodded to the two mining technicians.

"Now," he said. "The entrance to the catacomb is right over there,"

The two went away, carrying their bulky burden slung between them. Presently they came back again without it.

Trevor took his sun-stone from his pocket. Jen clutched his arm and cried, "No!"

"There's no danger now," he said. "He hasn't time enough left to do anything with me. And—I feel somehow that I should tell him—"

He put the sun-stone to his brow, and in his mind he cried, "Shannach!"

And into his mind came the cold, tremendous presence of the Last One. In an instant it had read Trevor's thoughts.

"So this is the end, Trevor?"

"Yes," Trevor said steadily. "The end."

He was braced for the wild reaction of alarm and passion, the attempt to seize his mind, to avert doom.

It didn't come. Instead, from the Last One, came a stunning pulse of gladness, of mounting joy.

"Why—why, you want me to do this?" Trevor cried.

"Yes, Trevor! Yes! I had thought that the centuries of waiting for death would be long yet, and lonely. But this, this will free me now!"

Dazed by surprise, Trevor slowly made a gesture, and their ship throbbed upward into the sky. Another gesture, and the technician beside him reached toward the key of the radio-detonator.

In that moment he felt the mind of Shannach crying out as in a vast, mingled music, a glad chorus of release against chords of cosmic sorrow for all that had been and would never be again, for the greatest and oldest of races that was ending.

The receding city below erupted flame and rock around the catacomb mouth as the key was pressed.

And the song of Shannach ebbed into silence, as the last of the children of mountains went forever into night.